# Not Your Child's Bedtime Stories

## By: MD-MAC

# NOT YOUR CHILD'S BEDTIME STORIES

*Do you ever take time to just read something nasty to your lover? Do something different and experience a different form of intimacy.*

*Each story is short to read so when you're done light a candle and get it on!*

*Most of us grew up reading nursery rhymes and fairy tales but I do not believe you have ever been introduced to this version.*

*These short stories have been reprised in their own way to bring your sexuality, your imagination and your orgasmic senses to a place where they have never journeyed before. As you lie in bed at night with the one you love read a story and allow your pleasures to soar, take flight and become absorbed in each other.*

# AUTOGRAPH PAGE

# TABLE OF CONTENTS

# ANSEL AND GRETAL

Ansel and Gretal had grown up together in a beautiful rural countryside their entire life. They were inseparable and even though they were not actually brother and sister they treated each other as if they were.

Ansel called Gretal's name from the grass below up to her window sill and asked her what she was doing. "Ansel I'm not doing anything, just fiddling

around with some things in my room." "You want to go for a walk Gretal?" "Sure" so Gretal grabbed her shawl and met Ansel at the front door. "Where are we going Ansel?" "Gretal lets be adventurous and take a walk in the woods down the way." "Ansel you know that woods is off limits, it's too dangerous." Gretal don't worry I will protect you. There is nothing to worry about I have always had your back." So Gretal went along with Ansel, as they got deeper into the woods Gretal started worrying about what would happen if they went too far. After about an hour Gretal was getting scared and Ansel kept reiterating to her that all was well and kissed her cheek.

This was the first time Ansel had done anything physical to Gretal. He liked the way she smelled and her skin was so soft. They were already holding hands but suddenly Ansel just pulled Gretal to him and he kissed her. His tongue latched onto to her as if they were two animals in heat. Gretal pushed him and said "Ansel what are you doing? We are not suppose too do things like that.

You are like a brother to me." Ansel apologized for his actions and asked her if it was okay for them to keep going deeper into the woods.

Gretal was okay with that so they continued until the came upon a cottage. This cottage was immaculate, flowers were planted all around the house, it was if the trees were singing in the sunshine. Approaching the cottage they noticed some pies sitting in the window sill cooling. They knocked on the door but no answer. Ansel turned the doorknob it was unlocked they proceeded to go in.

Everything in the cottage was neatly placed the food cooking smelled wonderful and the air in the room smelled so pleasant. Just then without any thought Ansel grabbed Gretal again and this time he slid his hand up her leg found his fingers in her shorts around her panties and straight up her pussy. "Ansel what are you doing." Gretal what do you think I'm doing, I'm sorry but I want you so bad. Let my fingers feel the softness of your pussy, it is getting wet, let me make you feel good, allow me to make you feel the way a woman wants to feel. I want to finger your pussy until you can't take no more and want my dick inside of you. Gretal do you want me? Tell me you want me. Your skin is so soft your cum is so thick, Gretal tell me you want me to taste you, tell me Gretal, tell me." Yes, yes, yes Ansel I want you, I want to feel your lips and tongue all over my body. I want you to taste my pussy. I want you to rub your body all over me. Yes Ansel yes."

They made their way back into the bedroom of the cottage unaware of the occupant who not only lived there but was watching them from the inside of her closet. Most people would have labeled this lady a witch but she was simply an outcast who chose to be left alone. Ansel and Gretal didn't even notice her.

As they lay on her bed that seemed as soft as a bag of giant marshmallows Ansel removed Gretal's clothing as if she were on fire and he could not wait to extinguish her. She removed his clothes in the same manner. It was as if time stood still and the lady standing in the closet was getting turned on as she stood and watched their next move.

Ansel's fingers and hand penetrated Gretal's pussy and it was beginning to throb. Her back was beginning to arch and the sounds coming out of her mouth would make any woodland creature want to fuck each other. Ansel whispered, "I am going to fuck you so good, you are going to beg me for more, you are going to want me to fuck you all the time. Don't worry I will take care of you." Gretal lay there and took his entire dick inside of her. She screamed in pleasure but also pain because she never had dick inside of her. She was squirting pussy juice all over his dick and the more she screamed the deeper he went. They never stopped to think the lady would be coming home or where she was.

The lady was still in the closet looking at Ansel and Gretal enjoy each other while her fingers were slowing moving down to her pussy and she found herself masturbating while watching them.

She glided her hand up to her titties squeezing them hard making her produce milk and even though she wanted to yell herself she kept it to a soft moan. Gretal was screaming so loud they never heard her moaning. The lady could only imagine how his dick would feel inside of her. She played with her pussy for as long as Gretal was getting fucked by Ansel and she loved it. Her pussy had never gotten this wet before and she wanted to thank them for making her afternoon a spectacular one.

After a few hours of Ansel fucking Gretal they collected their clothing and got ready to leave when they heard a noise coming from the closet it was a soft moan and groan. "Who's there?" said Ansel. He went to the closet door opened it looking at the lady of the cottage standing their fingering herself licking her cum off all at the same time. Ansel said, "We didn't know anyone was here, we apologize for trespassing." The lady didn't seem upset but she told them it's not nice to walk into someone's house without permission but since no one really knew she was out there she was not going to say anything but did ask a favor of Ansel. "Young man you and the young lady made me feel alive so I was wondering if you two wouldn't mind coming back in a few days and fucking each other again. I'd love to watch." Ansel was okay with it and talked Gretal into it as well.

As they were beginning to leave the lady turned to Ansel and said "oh yes I'm going to need you to lick the pussy juices off of me. I usually have young men for lunch but today I'm going to need you to eat me and I need you to eat me well." Ansel did what she wanted and when they left Gretal asked him "was her pussy better than mine?"

He said no but Gretal later found out that Ansel went to the cottage without her on most occasions and the lady in the cottage and Ansel were fucking each other so much with no shame she no longer

had young men for dinner but she in fact had become Ansel's main dish.

## BEAUTE' AND THE BEAST

It wasn't very often but every now and then I thought I would go out and experience the night life by having a drink and a small appetizer at a local bar I had frequently passed on my way to work.

I sat down to have my double shot of tequila with a twist of lemon and lime and in she walks. This beautiful woman that I have never seen before in my neighborhood walks in like she owns the place. It was as if time had stopped.

There she was a sexy, voluptuous woman that I anticipated in having and I would not stop until I got her. I invited her to sit down with me and while I didn't think I had a chance in hell to talk to her I remained confident and gave it my best shot.

We sat at the bar and as she drank her martini with a lime twist I could not help but look at her big beautiful legs, her titties that looked filled with the most healthy milk a baby could drink and her hips were as curvy as a road in the middle of nowhere so I could only imagine how wet her pussy could get and I wanted to get inside of her.

I looked up at the clock and realized that it was almost 3 am in the morning and we were still sitting there talking or maybe she was talking and I didn't hear a thing because I was too busy being in my own fantasy world imagining what lied beneath her clothing.

I looked at this beautiful lady in front of me and apologized to her for keeping her out so long. Time got away from her and I. I asked if I could walk her to her car, she obliged. As we walked along she asked if she could see me again. This time I obliged. What caught me off guard was the fact she asked me if I would follow her home. I was shocked I didn't know this woman and this was not the typical thing I would do when I went out to a bar. I thought about it but I turned her down. I did want to see her again and I wanted to get inside of her but I also wanted to get to know who she was as a person and did her inside match her outside. I hope it would.

We said our goodbyes and decided to meet at a small restaurant in 3 days. We didn't exchange numbers or addresses; I waited the 3 days and met her at the little restaurant on the corner. She was beautiful, more beautiful than the first time I met her. She had a blue dress on with these sexy high heels and it was making my dick hard as I was looking at her walk toward me.

I pulled the chair out so she could sit down and I couldn't help but look down her dress and see her cleavage pulsating up and down as she took a breath.

I was so turned on it was becoming very hard for me to stay a gentleman. By no means was I a perfect gentleman because my thoughts toward her were about getting right down nasty. I wanted to lick her pussy and taste her on my tongue and hear her scream in ecstasy however, I remained cool, calm, and collective.

The next thing I know I felt something in my middle of my pants. Something was pushing up against my dick and damn it was getting harder and harder and she was smiling at me knowing how it was affecting me. It was her foot. It was as if her toes were massaging my dick, it was feeling awesome which got me fantasizing about her and I even more.

I dropped my napkin on the floor and as much as I wanted her to keep going I needed her to stop. My napkin went under the table so I repositioned myself to pick up the napkin looked under the table to my napkin and saw that she did not have on any underwear. Her pussy was hanging out; she was dripping wet because as she was playing with my dick with her toes she was masturbating. I sat back up and she had the biggest smile on her face. She picked up a piece of bread off the table, took her finger swiped the butter wiped it across the bread and put it toward my mouth.

The piece was just the right size for my mouth. I tasted the butter with her juices on it and when she put it in my mouth her fingers went across my lips as well which allowed me to taste her pussy. It was delicious and I enjoyed it. It was the best piece of bread I had ever eaten. At this point I wanted to skip dinner and go straight to dessert. I was ready to tear her apart. But amazingly I remained cool all the way through dinner. I managed to strike up a no nonsense conversation with her. I felt as though I was just rambling because I was trying to keep my dick down and she wasn't helping my situation at all.

We had been at the restaurant so long I didn't realize we were the only ones left; we were sitting in a back corner secluded from everyone else. I had to zone out for a while because I was doing my best to keep a straight head and when I came back to myself Beaute' had disappeared. I was so upset with myself because she probably figured I wasn't paying any attention to her.

Then all of a sudden I felt something on my dick, I pulled up the tablecloth and there Beaute' was, she was on the floor on all fours sucking my dick and man did I want to let loose. She was slobbering all over my dick with her juicy soft lips while I just sat trying to maintain composure and ready to explode inside her mouth. The waiter came by and asked if I needed anything and I uttered out, "No, no, um no thank you, I'm fine. " Just as he walked away I felt like my balls pushed up straight into my dick and I exploded into Beaute's mouth. She stayed down there another 10 minutes and continued to lick the outer rim of my dick head and make me squirm even more.

I sat there and closed my eyes for a second and she reappeared just as quickly as she had disappeared. She sat up like a classy lady who had just stepped out of high class fashion magazine and acted as if nothing had happened. "That was amazing" whispering to Beaute'. She whispered back, "it was my pleasure." Then she said to me, "would you like to meet here every week, same place, and same time." Of course I said yes and after the 4th dinner date I finally asked her name and she said, "You know my name, I am the beast who walks in Beaute'."

# GOLDIE AND THE BEHRS

G rowing up was not easy for Goldie. She lived in a rural area where everyone knew everybody so people were always in each other's business. She lived in a two bedroom place with her mom, 3 brothers and stepfather.

She slept on the couch in the living room. She took up less space. While things were pleasant in the

home she always wanted to live in a place where she could have her own room and privacy.

She ran into a classmate 4 years after graduation and they became really good friends. She had known him since her sophomore year. They were talking one day and he asked her if she ever thought of moving out. She said yes but she was making the most out of her situation and continued to work and save money.

Well her friend Laney made her an offer she really didn't think she could refuse. She went home and discussed it with her mother and even though her mother did not approve she did want to hold Goldie back from making any decisions of her own even if she thought she was making a bad one.

Laney lived with his father and brother in a 3 bedroom house that was big enough to hold 5 more people if it wanted to. Anyway, Lance, Laney's brother was away at school and there was an extra bedroom for her if she wanted it. Laney's father was always out of town on business so Laney was home alone at least 85% of the time. He just wanted some company.

As it turns out he could not ask for a better roommate. They got along great, they treated each other like sister and brother and over 9 months life was great for the both of them and one night they went out to a club together. They were out of it, they had drunk so much they had to leave their car and call Uber to drive them home. They laughed and talked all the way home. They unlocked the door to go in the house as they normally did and Laney tripped over something. He wasn't sure what it was and didn't pay any attention. He went upstairs to his room. Goldie saw what he tripped over, it was a suitcase. She didn't think anything of it. She figured it was just Mr. Behr coming home from his business trip and he knew about Goldie living there.

She went to the bathroom off of her room and got undressed. She was built so beautiful. You see in school she was ridiculed so much by other students because of her weight but she got revenge by losing the weight and in spite of how she was treated she always kept a kind heart. She had to admit she was proud of the body she had worked hard for but refused to share it with anyone.

She climbed into bed as she always did and fell asleep. Sometime in the middle of the night she felt this hand caressing her breasts. It felt so good to her. She just lies there and kept her eyes closed as if she didn't know what was going on. All of a sudden she felt the warm mouth of someone's tongue licking and sucking on her nipples.

She tried to stay quiet but she couldn't help it, she moaned in ecstasy. Her back was starting to arch and her pussy was starting to get wet. She felt a hand move over her neck to her breasts down her stomach and touch her in her place of eruption. A finger was gliding over her clit and entering her pussy while another finger was reaching for the whole orgasmic glory. Goldie was losing her senses. She wanted to scream yet her quiet moans seemed to make whoever were with her move his fingers with more intensity.

As this persons fingers moved in and out of her it suddenly stopped. She wanted to open her eyes but didn't know who she was going to see so she kept them closed.  Just when she thought it was over someone turned her over and put something in her ass. It hurt her so bad she wanted to scream and she did in her pillow. She took the hurt feel good pain that was being injected into her. She came on herself so much it wetted her asshole so no lubrication was needed. She realized it was a dick going in and out of her and it was big.

It was growing inside of her like a joey in a pouch. She was enjoying each moment of what was happening to her. While this dick was inside of her, her pussy was pulsating, it was throbbing and it felt so good. Goldie softly spoke out and said, "Harder, deeper." That's just what happened, dick went harder and deeper. She had never been fucked before and for her first time she loved it.

Her ass was open as wide as the Grand Canyon and there was no turning back now.

She took every inch that was given to her; she didn't want anything going to waste. Of course by this time her high had worn off. She was taking all of it inside of her. He pulled her up to where he could fondle her breasts and squeezed them so hard she just knew she was going to holler. His dick was at the tip of her ass where he was only slightly going inside then he would thrust his dick hard inside of her. Her pussy was so wet she thought she peed on herself. He repeatedly kept doing this until he erupted inside of her ass making it look like her ass erupted like a volcano with white lava pouring out of it.

He did it, he came, he's satisfied; he got up and left the bedroom. She opened her eyes started to wonder who took that one thing that no one had ever felt. The next morning she went downstairs to breakfast and had no idea what to say. She saw Laney and said "good morning", she saw Mr. Behr and said "good morning". She was looking for clues to see which one may have entered her the night before and giving her the greatest physical pleasure she had ever come to experience.

To no avail, neither one of them said anything nor did their mannerisms change. She didn't know what to think. She went to bed that night wondering which one it was. She didn't want to say anything to Laney about it being his father and she didn't want to accuse it being Laney. She fell asleep around midnight but again was awaken to someone caressing her body.

His hands were caressing her breasts and felt what appeared to be a mouth down licking her pussy and all of sudden feeling his tongue goes inside her pussy. Her juices were flowing once again. It was hot, it was good and again as much as she wanted to open her eyes she couldn't do it. She took all that he wanted to give me. He never said a word he ate her pussy as if he were eating a medium well steak with a baked potato. The more she shifted her hips, the more his tongue rammed into her pussy eventually hitting her g-spot.

She was done, she couldn't hold back the pleasure she was feeling, she pulled her legs over her head and it felt as though his entire head was inside of her. Once again she creamed in a way she had never experienced. Shortly after that, she felt a dick move to her lips and the tip was wet and sticky. She knew he wanted her to put it in her mouth. Goldie had never sucked dicked but she thought she would give it a try. She was a natural.

She glided her tongue over his dick and licked his balls until he came on her face. He took the cum off her face with his fingers and rubbed it on her lips as if it was lip gloss.

She tasted what she had brought out in him. It was like the consistency of buttercream frosting but no taste she could describe. He got up and left the room and once again she kept her eyes closed until he left.

The next morning she went down to breakfast and once again she simply said "good morning Laney, good morning Mr. Behr." They both replied and once again no one gave her any inkling that it was him.

Shortly after that Lance walks in the door says good morning and tells Goldie "I've been here for two nights and have yet to sleep in my own bed." Neither one said anything to Laney or Mr. Behr and for the next 3 nights Lance was home he never did sleep in his bed but every night he went into his room and fucked Goldie as much and as hard as he wanted and she never opened her eyes but after that her eyes were wide shut.

## LIL BOY BLEU

Lil Boy Bleu was a quiet one who always stayed to himself. He didn't mind tending to the sheep and feeding the cows their daily corn so life as he knew it was content and he was not expecting anything else.

As Bleu was walking on his daily route to check on his animals he always passed a little house on the other side of the rural road but he never knew who lived there. It was a creepy looking house that was always dark and it seem as though it didn't have any life in it so it was never his intention to stop and ask anyone who lived there.

So for 30 straight days in July, Bleu did what he was required until one day his eyes met a girl dressed in a yellow dress with a white bonnet on her head. He said hello to the girl but she either didn't hear him or she totally ignored him so he did not think much of it and continued on with his daily chores.

As the day went by he ran into the girl again and this time she spoke to him. "Hello Bleu, how are you." "Hello" said Bleu in his soft spoken voice. He said, "I've never seen you before, where do you live." "I live in the creepy house that you pass every day. I sit on my tuffet eating my curds and whey when along comes a spider and sits right beside me and always frightens me away."

"I'm sorry to hear that, so what is your name?" "My name is Miss Muffet so every day they spoke to one another in passing but one day Miss Muffet asked Bleu what he did for fun. "I really don't do anything for fun, I don't have any time." "Bleu, all work and no play makes for a dull boy" so Bleu went home that night and thought about what Miss Muffet said and decided to see what he could do for fun.

The next morning Bleu saw Miss Muffet and told her he likes to run the fields and catch small rabbits for fun and then go out behind his haystack to sleep when he gets tired. Miss Muffet asked him to show her his haystack and he obliged.

When they got behind the haystack Miss Muffet lifted up her dress and jumped on top of Lil Boy Bleu. "Bleu my nickname is Little Miss Muffet but my titties are not little and I have this big wet pussy waiting on you. Bleu why do they call you Lil Boy Bleu? Your dick is so hard and big through your pants, can I see it? Take your dick out Bleu." Bleu did it with the quickness. He had never had pussy before and he was definitely old enough to know

what it was and what to do with it. He always kept himself super busy because his father left when he was young and his mother depended on him to run the farm.

His soft spoken voice quickly left and he said to Miss Muffet, "I have been waiting on your sweet ass for days but I was waiting on you to make the first move but now I'm going to tell you what else you need to do. Get down on your knees as quick as you can and put my dick in your mouth and suck it like I know you can and when you are done lay on your back because I'm going to slurp the cum out your pussy just like that and when I'm done licking up and down on you I'm going to roll you over and stick my dick inside of you like a bull does a cow and if you have to moo, moo your ass off loud because I'm going to make you cum from sun up to sun down."

So that's what Bleu did every day after chores he fucked Miss Muffet on that haystack in a way she has never been fucked before.

After he was done Miss Muffet went home and ate her curds and whey and Boy Bleu layed out on the haystack with a piece of straw in his mouth going over what had went on that day. Smiling to himself and grabbing his dick and saying "wait until tomorrow I'm going back down on that bitch."

# LIL RED FROM THE HOOD

Nobody ever knew her real name no one knew where she came from. This lady just showed up one day out of nowhere. All anyone knew was she went by the name of Lil Red and she was straight from the hood.

The thing about Lil Red from the hood was that she was very articulate when she spoke. She was smart, beautiful, kind but she was also hard in a

way that if you said something to her she didn't quite like she would definitely let you know where you stood with her.

She was out taking her walk one day when she was approached by a man she had never seen before. She really didn't feel like talking and she politely told him, "Sir I don't know you, don't care to know you." Lil Red kept it moving. This man was quite persistent. He did not take no for an answer. Now Lil Red had to admit to herself that he was a handsome man but she had been through too much to realize that looks were not everything.

As days went by Lil Red took her daily walk on the same path and always at different times. It seemed no matter what time she went on her daily walk she was approached by this man. She was beginning to wonder if he just hid out in the bushes and waited on her.

It was a Saturday afternoon about 70 degrees and out pops this man in front of her. She looked at him and said, "damn what are you a wolf waiting to pounce on his prey." He smiled at her and said, "yes mamn, I am. I'm waiting on you. Now don't get me wrong I do find you very attractive but its more than that.......I just want to get to know who you are."

Lil Red looked at him again, smiled and politely said, "sir I am not interested in you or your interest in me." She walked by him as he stood there and as usual she kept it moving.

Two weeks went by, then six weeks went by. She didn't see the man walking on her path. She was a little curious about what happened to him but she just kept it moving as she always did. After about two to three months she was walking down a new path that had been constructed and ran into this man sitting on the bench. Lil Red was going to walk on by but decided to stop and say hello. "How

you doing sir, it's been a while since I've seen you. How have you been?" He looked up at her and said, "Doing well thank you for asking. I wanted to walk where you were but after you called me a wolf I decided I would not bother you anymore. I didn't want you to think I was stalking you, I didn't want you afraid of me." "I'm not afraid I just didn't feel real comfortable about what you were doing." "I understand" replied the man. "What is your name sir?" My name is Kenneth. "What's your name?" I simply go by Lil Red. "Lil Red, huh…..interesting little lady." "Well Kenneth it was nice meeting you maybe I will run into you again." "Well Lil Red maybe I will run into you tomorrow say around 4 o'clock."

The next day at exactly 4pm Lil Red met Kenneth at the bench from the previous day and they sat there and talked until dusk and they did this for weeks. Addresses were never given out, phone numbers were not exchanged and even though they were getting to know one another neither one wanted to infringe on the others private life.

One warm day in the fall Lil Red came to the bench where they met on a daily basis and she wanted to share something with him. She wasn't sure how he would respond so she wrote it down in spoken word to see how he would receive it. Kenneth sat down she looked into his eyes and was ready to share these words with him. Before she said anything he was looking deep into her eyes leaned in and gently kissed her on the lips. He said, "There is something I want to say to you, I didn't quite know how so I did it in spoken word." She couldn't believe it. He said, "can I tell you what I wrote", Lil Red said yes.

- You see when I first laid eyes on you the intensity of your body instantly made my nature rise but when I started conversing with you, you made my eyes wide.

- My eyes got wide to what I really see inside of you. Something so warm, gentle and kind but a fire so strong the heat cannot be denied
- Bringing me strength in a way you will never know something that even the smartest constituents can't even unfold
- Putting a desire in me that the thrust of my mind cannot wrap around
- I just know that if I have get you inside of me you will have my mind, body and soul

I like you Lil Red and even though I want to see every inch of you standing in front of me naked, dripping in your own juices I don't want to jeopardize the friendship we have established. Lil Red was feeling the exact same way. She didn't know what to say she was speechless.

Lil Red lived in a little cabin not too far off the path so she asked Kenneth if he would come with her. He agreed and they went to her cabin. Once inside she looked at him and said absolutely nothing. She simply took off her clothes, Kenneth looked at her and said, " Lil Red what beautiful breasts you have…..more for you to kiss. Lil Red what a beautiful clit you have….more for your tongue to lick……Lil Red what a beautiful ass you have……..more for your dick to fuck. Lil Red what a big mouth you have…..better for me to suck. Lil Red what a long tongue you have….better for me to lick. Lil Red what big eyes you have….better for me to watch. Lil Red what big hips you have…..better for you to hold. Lil Red you got all that body…..just more for you to cum……cum in me on me just give it to me the way I want it because the fire in me is so strong it's going to take all you got to put me out.

You see in actuality the wolf wasn't Kenneth it was Lil Red. She put it on him all night long until

Kenneth was not dead but sound asleep like a baby in a basinet and she decided that she wanted to have a real relationship with this man she met walking on her path months prior. He woke up and smiled at her she leaned in and gently kissed him on the lips and she started to speak. What did she say? Well that's another story!

# PETE AND TINK

The island of Everland had always been filled with the lost boys along with Pete and Tink. It was a peaceful place that most lost boys never wanted to leave but after years of entertaining the lost boys and Pete Tink found herself in a place where she wanted more. She always had a special place in her heart for Pete now she wanted to feel Pete's Pete inside of her bell.

She was tiny but beautiful and longed for one wish, the one wish where she could be the size of Pete. You see the fairies and Pete never aged. They never got old, they reached a certain level in appearance and stayed there until the fairies wings were cut off and they would die but Pete was immune to old age in Everland. For years Tink has seen Pete in all his glory and she wanted a piece of the action. Pete did not stop to think that Tink would get excited over him taking off his cloth that covered his giant dick or while he masturbated in front of her while looking at a picture of Wendie.

Tink was flying on one side of the island that would remind someone of the bayou and ran across an old game. It was an old Atari set with a set of joysticks. Tink decided she wanted to see if it worked so she sprinkled a little pixie dust on it to see if it would come on and to her delight it did. She picked the joystick up and all she could do was visualize wrapping her hand around Pete's dick and stroking it the way she had watched him. At that moment something was changing inside of her. She grew excited, her little pussy was starting to tingle but more than that she grew big. She was a life size Tink, the same size as Pete. She was so excited, she really didn't know how it happened and she didn't care she just knew she could not waste any time in case she went right back to her normal size.

She grabbed the game up in her arms and took flight. Her wings were so bright they lit up the sky and it was hard to tell what it was until she got closer. The lost boys saw her and they could not believe their eyes. When she landed 2 of the lost boys were standing there in total disbelief. "Tink is that you?" said the first lost boy. He started salivating at the mouth. She stood there in her two piece outfit with half of her titties hanging out and ready to be sucked. Every part of her body looked perfect. The lost boy was ready to be found and suck on her titties so he asked her. "Tink can I suck your titties, they look so good, please Tink." Surprisingly she said yes. He walked up to her opened his mouth and put his mouth on the softness of her skin. He started sucking gently then it got harder and all of a sudden she started letting out whimpers of ectasy. It was feeling so good to her. The 2nd lost boy standing there was starting to get a hard dick and all he could think about doing to Tink was pulling down her bikini bottoms and sticking his tongue in her wet fairy pussy. The 2nd lost boy did not even bother to ask because he saw how Tink was engulfed in what was happening to her by the first lost boy. He got on his knees pulled down her bikini bottom and stuck his tongue straight in her pussy. She hollered and kept repeating yes over and over again. She had never experienced anything so good before and even though she enjoyed the lost boys sucking her titties and eating her pussy she still longed for Pete. She wanted to save the true penetration for him.

While all of this was going on other fairies were flying by not really paying attention what was going on even Pete flew by but he didn't think anything of it because he was used to catching the lost boys performing some sexual acts on a life size inflatable woman they had in their hut. After about an hour she was exhausted, she was worried that she wouldn't be able to feel the pleasures of Pete's Pete. The 2 lost boys fell asleep right where they stood with the biggest smile on their faces.

Tink decided to move on to see if she could find Pete. It was taking her longer than expected because of the sexual acts performed on her it was making her wings smaller. She was so used to flying she could not believe how long it was taking to walk. She could have been to Pete's hut in 10 minutes compared to 2 hours of walking but by this time she was so excited. Her body was on fire and she couldn't wait to see Pete.

She went up the steps and quietly called Pete's name. "Pete are you in there, Pete it's Tink." Tink called his name again and this time she heard him say something. "Tink is that you? Where have you been, I have been looking for you all day." "Something amazing happened to me Pete, I want to show you." "Sure Tink come on in." Tink walked into the hut and Pete could not believe his eyes. "It was you, it was you I saw the lost boys all over, Tink what did you do?" Tink sat down and explained what happened to her earlier in the day. She didn't know if Pete would want her after he said he saw her with the lost boys so she decided to take a chance and tell him what was on her mind. "Pete we have been friends forever and the one thing I always wanted to do with you was to fuck you, I want to feel your dick on the inside of my wet fairy pussy, I just want you to take me and do whatever you want."

Pete really had never given this a lot of thought so he asked Tink to hold on and said he would be right back. She was baffled by this but she waited for him to come by. After about 10 minutes Pete was back with the 2 lost boys he saw her with earlier. "Tink I want you to finish what you started with these 2 lost boys." Tink couldn't believe it she wanted Pete. Tink was heartbroken, she knew she made a mistake and she felt smaller than she ever had. Tink looked at Pete and said "no Pete I don't want them, I want you, I want you to touch me and kiss me and lick me all over, please Pete please." (sobbing). Pete picked her up and put her on his bed, he took off her tiny outfit which only covered her pussy and nipples removed his loin cloth and started kissing her lips, neck, chest, nipples, stomach, and found his tongue in her wet soggy pussy. His dick was huge, it was throbbing in pain though it seemed because he wanted to ram it inside of her at that moment.

Pete felt something ignite on the inside of him and just then he rammed his dick inside of her pussy and rode her hard, so hard that she felt like she was floating on air in the form of pleasure and pain. He beat her pussy up then flipped her over and rammed his dick in her pussy from behind. She was hollering in delight. He had both of them on their knees and he was fucking her so hard and so strong she didn't believe he would ever cum. After 2 hours of Pete fucking Tink's pussy he came in her so much it was running down her legs. By this time the small wings that Tink had were gone. Pete had done what Tink wanted. He fucked the wings off of her and she loved it. Pete looked at Tink when he got done and said, "Tink, I had never thought about fucking you but when you turned down the lost boys this time and begged me to put my dick in you I could not resist, your pussy was so good, so wet." I'm going to fuck you again and I want you to take it. "Can you take it Tink?" "Yes, oh yes Pete, I can take it." He fucked her on and off for the rest of the night.

She never wanted it to end but it did. When she awoke the next morning she was back to her normal size. She really didn't know how long her wish would last but she held onto it as long as she could. Pete awoke as well to find Tink flying right above him smiling so big. "Tink you were the best, in all these years I never would have thought your fairy pussy would be so good. I hope we can do it again one day." "So do I Pete you made my wish come true." Tink flew off to start her day to see what others fantasies were out there waiting for her.

# P NOK

I was created by Sam in the lower east side called the northern lights at a time where the wind howled and you could barely walk outside.

At some point in my existence I realized that I wasn't like the other children running around the neighborhood. I was stiff, my legs and arms didn't

bend like everyone else but I had a nose on me that was like no other.

Actually I didn't realize how my nose would grow until after I told a lie to my Dad and once I told the truth it would go back down. Still I was ridiculed and bullied by others because I was not considered real and no one wanted to be my friend until one day I met someone that would change my life and open my marble eyes to something brand new.

The name was Mae and she was a caramel complexion with a smile so bright it lit up a room. I so wished I was a real boy. Anyway, we started hanging out and became really good friends and by the end of the school year we were enjoying each other company every day.

It wasn't long after this that we started experimenting with each other; she knew I was not flesh and blood but she liked to be touched down there. I didn't know what it was, I had never seen one but I was curious as well.

She took my little wooden hand and moved it down there and asked me to move my hand around to stir her up. I did and even though I wasn't getting any feeling I saw that she was enjoying it quite a bit. I realized that my hand was absorbing moisture and my hand was turning white. I had no idea what that was, I thought something was wrong.

She explained to me and said, " P Nok, that is me cuming on myself. I am ejaculating from my pussy and its making me wet." She moaned in a way I have never heard and then she asked me to fuck her. I didn't know what this meant. She told me that it was me putting my wooden part in her pussy and making her feel good except Sam did not give me a dick. I have never pissed in my life. I'm wooden for goodness sakes. I had an idea.

I asked Mae to ask me a question. I told her to ask me if I was a real boy. "P Nok, are you a real boy?" I replied with a yes. "P Nok, are you a real boy?" Yes, I replied, As I lied my nose began to grow and

I could tell it was turning her on. I just wanted to hear her moan over and over again. It really couldn't do anything for me but I could certainly tell it was doing something to her,

"P Nok I want you to put your nose in my pussy and roll it around in there and then move in and out like you are churning butter, go up and down". I did what she told me and every time I pulled out to go back in with my nose it just kept getting whiter and wetter. I had no idea how long I was doing it because again I wasn't feeling anything nor was I tired.

By this time her moans had changed to hollering. She was yelling saying, "don't stop, keep going, deeper P Nok deeper." All of a sudden she let out a scream I had never heard and I looked at her to see if she was okay. She had the biggest smile on her face, she was lying in all this cum as she called it and everything was wet. My nose was so wet I didn't know what to do.

She got up and got something to wipe my nose and then she used a blow dryer to dry it. I was so happy I could help her and I helped her all most everyday all summer long. All of a sudden going back to school after summer break was sad and exciting. Mae told all of her friends what I did to her over the summer and they were curious as well. So every day after school I would meet with one of Mae's friends and told them to ask me a question and I would tell a lie and within 5 minutes I had my nose in their pussy. All of a sudden the boys wanted to be friends because they noticed all the girls being around me. I had found my quest in life.. I could do it for hours on end but realized they couldn't so I asked them what that hole in the back was for. That of course is a different story.

## PUSS-N-BOOTS

It was as if I had travelled back in time. I sensed I was not in the same time as you or the same century. I had awaked to two men standing over me staring at me wondering if I was alive or dead. I was very much alive but I was wondering, "how did I get here." "What is your name, where did you come from, how did you get here." These questions just kept coming at me from both of these men. I didn't have any answers to any of these because I was wondering myself.

Three days prior I was working out in fencing class when I suddenly felt very light headed so I sat there until I felt better and went back to business as usual. After class I ran home to clean up so I could meet some friends out at a local bar. It was a little chilly so I wore my thigh high 5" platform boots with some jeans, a black off the shoulder top and a little leather jacket. I was feeling cute and pretty sexy. It was not unusual for me to go without panties so this night was not any different. I remember meeting my girlfriends having some shots and appetizers and this was all I remembered.

I wake up in a place that is unfamiliar to me. So I started asking questions like ,"what day is it, where am I, who are you." As I was asking questions I realized my ass and titties were hanging out. The only thing I had on were my boots. Where was I? I wanted answers and I wanted them quick. The two men claimed that they removed my clothing because they feared my clothes were contaminated but when I asked about why they leave my boots on they had not explanation. I wanted to talk to someone who had the answers. As the men left the room they informed me they would be sending in Mr. D who could answer all my questions.

Mr. D arrived a few minutes after they walked out. He was a broad shoulder dark hair man with thick eyebrows and thick mustache. He was tall and walked with a small limp to his left leg. He was handsome. He looked so familiar to me. I was getting ready to speak when he stopped me told me who he was and where I was. I was in the 18th century in Scottish territory. When I asked Mr. D why didn't he remove my boots he explained they were not sure if I was a prostitute because if women wore knickers they were considered prostitutes or women with immoral values.

"Ok Mr.D is this why you have me tied down. You think I'm a prostitute." On the contrary my dear lady you are quite lovely and I would like very much to thrust myself into in at this very moment. I looked down and the bulge under his jacket was quite large. As I lay there with anticipation and with my urgency I taught him some new words looked at Mr. D in his face and asked "does the D stand for Dick because it is quite big. What are you waiting on get over here and fuck me. Stick your dick in me and fuck me Mr. D."

He walked closer to me I took his hand and guided his hand to my pussy. I wanted him to feel how wet my pussy was. I took his finger glided it over my clit the more he rubbed my clit the wetter I got. So I thought I would go a step farther. I asked him to put his tongue on my clit. He acted appalled but curious all at the same time. He acknowledged this was something he had never done but always wanted to. I asked him to untie my wrists, he would not do it at first. I asked him again, he did. I grabbed him on the top of his head and pushed it down to my hot pussy that was anxiously waiting for his tongue. He went down stuck out his tongue started licking across my clit so hard it was not feeling good at all. I asked him to go slow take the tip of your tongue and gently go over my clit. Once he did that I was cumming all over the place.

As he did that I asked him to stick his finger in my pussy as it got all wet I asked him to put his wet finger in his mouth so he could taste me. He enjoyed it more than I thought because he licked my pussy so long I was ready to pass out. Mr. D was rising and I was ready. He pulled down his pants and rammed his dick into my wet hot pussy and I hollered out in ecstasy. He was on top of me slamming his dick into me as if he had never had pussy before. He exploded inside of me. He was out of control.

He then took his dick while he was still hard and came again except right before he came he took his dick out of me and came all over my face. He took his hands wiped my face scooping his cum then rubbing it all over my titties. Just as quick as he did this his dick was back inside of me exploding in me once more. His cum dripped out of my pussy running down toward my ass. My entire body was soak and wet. Mr. D's cum was all over me. When he got finished I asked him not to tie my wrists back up. He refused but he gave me a sponge bath when he was done leaving me on the table until the next morning.

The next morning was even more intense. I was still sleep when he came in the door awakened by his dick being shoved into my pussy once more. After he finished fucking my pussy he pressed a button on the wall which moved the table in a position where I was laying on my stomach. I could not see what he was doing but felt his dick ram inside of my asshole. I screamed so loud.

It was so painful but as he moved up and down on me like a frog on a lily pad it became less painful and more pleasurable. Mr. D went on for what seemed like hours. I realized I had become his own personal sex toy. He was thrusting his dick inside of me as if he was fencing.

I was already dreading for the next morning to come because I had nothing left. Maybe I bit off more than I could chew. I was ready for it to be over. Once again Mr. D walked into the room and all I could get out was the word no. I could not take not anymore dick from him. Everything on my body was sore. I just wanted him to let me go. Then I said it, "Let me go, let me go." I didn't holler I just said it in a small calm voice. Mr. D said "you could have left when you first got here." I didn't understand what he meant.

Just then I heard a voice calling me telling me to come back. It just kept speaking the words "come back." In a flash I raised up off my back sweating profusely trying to establish where I was. My eyes opened and I was attached to wires which monitored my vitals. I was in the hospital. I remember going out having fun with my friends but what I didn't know what happened after that. I was just grateful my friends were there but more so I was happy to wake up from my dream state. I enjoyed Mr. D but he almost took me out in my

coma like state. I was Puss-N-Boots for 3 days but I was glad to wake up being me again.

# SINDERELLA

inderella was on her way to womanhood. She was turning 21 in a few days and she was ready to go out and party as if there was no tomorrow. Now I wish that I could tell you that her childhood was filled was all kind of love and understanding. Well, for the most part it was. It came from the father who raised her since she was 5 years old.

Sinderella lived with her mom. It was just the 2 of them but life as a little girl was great. As a matter of fact it was great when her mom met her future husband. Life was good up until the age of 15 and life suddenly changed. Her mom passed away and it was just her, her step-father and the 2 half-sisters Sinderella referred to as Slut and Bitch. They were a result of his encounter with his first wife. They were bratty and spoiled and Sinderella didn't care if they went and played on a highway or back road. She could not stand them and they could not stand her.

Nevertheless she did not allow the strife to interfere with her kind heart or the fun she planned on having in the upcoming days. Her step-father was the only father she ever really knew but after her Mom passed his sadness overwhelmed him and he didn't pay any attention to any of them for a long time. It even took Sinderella a moment to regain her and who she was. It was something her mother put in her, strength and determination. Her birthday was coming up and with all strength she was going to try and disregard the dumb shit she knew her step-sisters would say to her and the strength to not fuck them up.

Sin's steps used to be beautiful and classy but some years of abuse from a little too much of everything left them looking run down and run over. The sad part was they were only 7 and 8 years older than her.

Sin searched through her closet to find something cute to wear out and she did. She looked at Chloe, her pet igauana and said, " Chloe I think this outfit is the one." She put it up to her and was looking in the mirror when Millicent the slut walked by. "Damn Sin you look like a cow in that outfit. Where you going?" "Millie you know where I'm going, you know what day it is." "Oh yea, it's your birthday or some shit, whatever, you are going to have an awful time. Don't know why you are wasting your time. All the men that are going to be there, well I probably fucked them all." "Yea I bet you did Slut. That's why your titties look like udders. Millie I'm not a little girl anymore so don't get fucked up ok." Millie threw her hand up as if to say whatever and walked out of her room with her nose in the air.

Sin kept looking through her clothes when Madison came by. "What you doing hole?" "Well if you must know you nosy bitch, I am looking for something to wear to this party." "Look hole, you are not built with hips, ass or titties so what do you think you are going to do tonight?" "None of your business bitch, so please get the fuck out of my room."

Sin found the outfit she was looking for turned around looked and Chloe and said, "this is it Chloe, I got it." She was all set to go. She went into her Dad's bedroom where he was lying in bed gave him a hug and kiss and let him know how much she loved him. He whispered, "thank you Sin, Happy Birthday, I love you." Sin was walking down the steps where Millie and Madison were waiting. She just knew they had something up their sleeve in which they always did which was usually a condom. "Oh Sin", said Millie "don't you looked fucked up in that outfit." "Oh Sin", said Madison you won't get no play with that outfit. You don't look slutty enough." Shaking her head, Sin was determined not to fuck them up. The last 5 years with them had been hell and she was ready to unleash a good down home ass whooping on them.

As she approached her car she noticed them looking at her through the window but she pretended she did not see them. She went to start her car and it wouldn't start. She instantly knew they had done something to it. Sin could have figured out what they did to her car because she was mechanically inclined and they were just stupid but she knew she would not make it to the party so she called a friend who lived down the street to see if he would give her a ride. Theodore and Sinderella had been friends for years and even though he had an on again off again girlfriend they remained friends through all the ups of downs of life.

Theodore drove up in an older car that her step-sisters would have never been seen dead in but it didn't matter to Sinderella. As far as she was concerned he was her Prince Charming just for coming to pick her up.

"Theo, thanks for coming to pick me up, I'm sure the slut and bitch had something to do with my car not starting. It's okay I'm determined to not let them put a damper on my evening. Where's Ms. Lace? (giggling to herself) I'm sorry Theo but is that all she wears? Anything she wears is always so lacey, but its ok she is just being herself I suppose. Thank you for dropping me off at the party, I should be able to catch a ride home with one of my girlfriends." "You're welcome and if you don't call me."

Theo dropped Sin off at the party and it was just what she imagined when she walked in the door. Everybody was having a good time. She saw around 20 people she knew but nobody she was really close to. She danced for a while had a few cocktails and even sat down at the bar and started chatting with this handsome man who turned out to be an ass and of course had fucked Millie.

After about 3 hours in the place she was ready to go home. She ended up calling Theo but no answer. She decided to walk it wasn't far to the bus stop. As she was walking she noticed a motorcycle ride pass her 3 different times. The 4th time it stopped and asked her if she needed a ride home. She said, "No, I'm walking to bus stop." "Come on Sinderella let me take you home." "Who are you? How do you know my name?" "I know you and know all about you" said the strange man who was dressed in jeans, a white shirt with a leather jacket and helmet. "Get on Sinderella." "I can't ride I have on a skirt." "Pull it up, I won't see anything." She agreed, did what he said and got on the back.

As they were riding down the street she noticed he was going slow and she was ready to get home. He said, "I'd like to take you on the ride of your life. Can I?" Sin had never done anything like this, she had never had sex so she said ok.

When she said ok it was as it the motorcycle instantly stopped. The strange man got off, took her hand, lead her to a tree, leaned her up against it and said, "now, take off your panties." She hesitated, he said it again "take off your panties." She did, then he said, "close your eyes." She did and when she did she felt something warm go into the inside of her pussy. It was his tongue. She was ready to rip the bark off the tree. He drove his tongue into her pussy that was now becoming soaked with her cum and she suddenly climaxed into his mouth. She had never done this before.

He said, " keep your eyes closed and hold on." He knew she had something left in her. He turned her around so she faced the tree. Just then she felt something go deep into her tight wet pussy from behind. She was screaming in pain and pleasure while at the same time she yelled, "go deeper." He did, her pussy was so wet it was running down her legs and he was rubbing his cum all over her ass. He said, "keep your eyes closed." She did. "I'm going to fuck you pass midnight Sinderella and I promise you , you will not be a pumpkin anymore. The strange man fucked her so long and so hard she felt like her legs were going to give out. When he was done he asked her to leave her panties off so her cum would be all over his motorcycle seat so she did.

He said goodnight and dropped her off at home. She never even saw his face. As she was collecting herself Theo was driving down the street and asked Sin if she had a good time. She said, "I was taken on the ride of my life." Theo replied back and said, "I know."

## Sleeping Beaute'

Sleeping Beaute' grew up in a small town and was raised by her father on their farm. They raised cattle and sheep. She learned how to shear sheep and sell their wool for even trade of materials they needed to survive. She loved her father but she yearned for more. She wanted someone to love and she wanted someone to love her back.

She was in her room one night lying in bed and she just wondered what the touch of a man felt like. She fell asleep and the next morning she heard some noise outside. Her father was outside talking to a gentleman around her age who was dropping off some wood for her father to build a shed and this young man was going to help him.

She gazed out the window looking at his strong arms, the way his biceps moved and the way his chest seemed to go up and down in slow motion. She found herself staring at him wanting him in a most passionate way.

She was starting to get moist and realized her hand was starting to move down into her panties. She was still looking out the window staring at him but what she didn't realize was that he had noticed her noticing him and he was staring back at her as well.

He watched her glide her hand down into her place of warmth and before she realized it she was masturbating and was doing it while he was watching. Her spell was broken when she heard her father come into the house and call her name. She never realized the young man was looking at her.

Her father asked her to come down stairs so she could meet the young man who was going to help him build the shed and asked her if she would prepare lunch. She said yes.

She made some soup and sandwiches and took them outside to them after 2 hours of working and while she went on as if nothing happened the young man found himself staring at her out of the corner of his eye and all he could think about was getting in between her legs and giving her the best pleasure ever. He was becoming consumed with her. His loins were rising and he was getting hot. He excused himself from the table and said he was going back to work because he couldn't take looking at her and the thoughts that were running through his head.

She excused herself as well, took the dishes back into the house while her father left to go to a neighbor's house to borrow a few tools and said he would be back shortly.

She wanted to go around to the shed and talk to this man but she said she better not because her father would be coming back soon. As she was cleaning off the table the young man walked up and started talking to her.

They told one another their names and started having a conversation. It was on his mind so he said it, "I noticed you looking at me from your upstairs window and I also noticed you pleasuring yourself. I wondered if I could take on where you left off."

Sleeping Beaute' had a look on her face as if she didn't know what he was talking about. She tried to keep calm and not let on that his voice was so sexy to her. It intoxicated her as if she was drinking wine. He walked up to her close enough to press his lips onto hers and she just froze in time.

She sniffed his scent from where she stood and wanted to touch him. Smelling him was setting her body on fire. He took his hand, slid it down her thigh and started gliding it back up underneath her skirt and found her place of pleasure. He gently grazed his finger across her panties but she wanted him to put his finger inside of her. She wanted to know what it felt like. Her breathing was starting to intensify and she was losing her focus realizing that she may melt right there on the spot.

He kept his hand down there for a few minutes but it seemed like hours to her. He took his hand from underneath her skirt and gently kissed her on the cheek. He told her that he wanted her. He wanted to take her to a place of ecstasy and wanted to give her the time of her life that she would always remember.

Just as he turned to walk away her father was coming up the road in his truck. The young man was back by the shed by the time her father reached the house. She was left standing overwhelmed and excited. She wanted him so bad she could taste him.

All of a sudden she heard this loud noise and she woke up. Her panties were wet, her clit was hard and all she could imagine is what would have happened if she stayed in her dream state and didn't wake up when she did.

Maybe she will have another dream tonight and she will get the pleasure she is seeking!

# THE PRINCESS WHO WAS A FROG

Ladd was playing outside one day with his silver ball that is mother had given him as a child. He decided to take it in the forest and toss it around hoping he would see something exciting.

As he was playing his ball hit a rock fell down the side of a cliff and rolled off into a small shallow lake that was inhabited by what looked like hundreds of lily pads. He ran down the path and found the pond. On the side of one lily pad sat a frog looking right up at him. Ladd didn't know that this frog could speak so he just sat there talking out loud. "Little frog I wish you could understand what I am saying. I lost my ball in this pond and I don't know how to get it back." It was quiet for about 30 seconds before he heard a soft voice say, "I can help you." "Who is that, where is that voice coming from." "Look down here, the frog sitting down here looking at you, I can help you. I can find your silver ball."

"Please, please find my silver ball. I will do and give you anything if you find it. No matter what it is I will do for you." As Ladd pleaded the frog had already found the ball and brought it to shore. "Did you mean what you said, you would give and do anything if I found it" said the frog. Yea I mean it whatdaya want said Ladd in this smug tone. All of a sudden Ladd's tone changed as if this frog owed him when it in fact helped him. The frog said "I want you to look at things differently, change your perspective because things are not always what they seem and never judge anything or anybody by outside appearances. Learn to be grateful do something nice for someone and you can start with me." Well Ladd was not trying to hear all this nonsense. He said "whatever" and started walking away.

The frog started jumping to him and yelling as loud as it could, "I want you to feed me, I want you to be my friend, and I want you to cuddle up to me at night when you're sleeping." Ladd just kept walking and didn't pay it any attention, he didn't even say thank you.

The frog showed up that evening tapped on the door and Ladd answered. He stood there looking as if he forgot what this frog had done for him. The frog spoke to him again and told him "you can have riches, and fame, but your word is your bond and that is more priceless than anything. You are almost a grown man still playing with a ball your mother gave you as a baby when you should be letting a woman play with your balls. What is wrong with you? You are not all that, you need to get over yourself. You can find someone to love you care about you and give you what you are missing. You are the only one who can make yourself happy but you can have someone in your life to add to your happiness."

Ladd was actually listening this time and over the next couple of months Ladd and the little frog became friends. He started cuddling up to it at night and enjoyed the company of having something to talk to even though it was just a frog.

One night has they were in bed Ladd noticed something different with the frog. It didn't cuddle it moved down to his dick and all of a sudden he felt this warm sensation engulf his dick and it started throbbing in a way it never had before.

All of a sudden Ladd exploded in a way he never had. Cum went everywhere. He didn't know what to think or what to do so he lies there and simply enjoyed it and pretended he was sleep. The frog however knew he was awake.

While his eyes were closed he suddenly realized that his dick was no longer engulfed the same way it was previously. It felt different and even though he had a good idea what it was he didn't want to speculate. He slowly openly his eyes and to his amazement he saw a beautiful lady with a gorgeous smile gazing in his eyes. He thought to himself how could this be? His thought was real. She had put Ladd's dick in her pussy and she was gently going up and down on him. His dick was throbbing and getting harder and deeper.

It was feeling so good to Ladd that he simply enjoyed and exploded in continuous bliss. It was warm then it got hot and he could feel her nectar rolling down on his dick and all he wanted to do was taste her. He decided to take charge and guided her up to his mouth and her pussy was covered with his lips. His tongue began to move over her clit where it stood strong. The more his tongue went over her clit the more she tensed up and started moaning. She continued to moan with a high level of pleasurable sensation. Her nectar was sweet more sweet than the strawberries that grew in his backyard. He tasted her, he licked her, he swallowed her and the more he did it the more he knew she wanted it. He was not going to stop until he knew she had enough. After some time they were both exhausted. Lying there in all their wetness sticking to one another like glue feeling satisfied more than anyone could imagine.

He wondered where she came from so he asked her who are you? Why Ladd I'm the woman you have always dreamed of having in your bed, I'm the one you always wanted. You always dreamt of eating my pussy, you dreamt of me sucking your dick. You wanted your dick sucked so long and so hard yet gently all at the same time. You wanted to thrust your dick in my pussy and make me cum. You wanted to feel my breasts rub all over you. You wanted to take your tongue and bring me to place of delight. You wanted me cum on your face.

You wanted to taste me. You wanted me to show you pleasure in a way you had never known and I have answered your dream.

Ladd it's time for me to go, I have answered your dream and it's time for me to return to the lily pond from which I had come.

Ladd said to her, "I thought you were a princess", she said, "I am a princess, a princess frog but now I bid adue but don't worry Ladd you will be fine, because I've left no warts on you."

# JACK AND JILL

There was a steep hill on the side of a high rock formation that generated the best spring water that anyone could every drink. Years prior someone had built a well at the top of this steep hill so that anyone who wanted water could draw it out with the bucket that was attached to the rope on the well.

One day Jack was approaching the steep hill to climb when he halfway up he noticed Jill bending over the well. Jack's dick began to get hard. He wanted to maintain his composure and when he arrived at the top of the hill he said hello to Jill. "Hmmmm, hi Jill how are you today." " I'm doing good Jack how are you?" It was almost impossible for Jack to keep his dick down because he could not stop staring at Jill. Jill was sexy to him. She had on a red plaid shirt that was unbuttoned so low it was showing the top part of her titties.

Her white shorts were cut so high into her ass he didn't know if she was wearing shorts or a thong because he could see the imprint of her pussy and all of her ass when she was bent over the well. Jack was off fantasizing about Jill when suddenly Jill said, "so Jack are you going to fetch a pail of water or are you going to stand there all day staring at my titties?"

Jack was a little embarrassed at first and then said to her, "well Jill if you don't want me to stare at your titties you shouldn't wear a shirt like that." "Well Jack maybe I wore it because I knew you were coming. I have to get back home but I have to walk back up here this evening to get more water. Would you help me Jack?" " I don't mind Jill, stop by my house on the way and I will just walk with you instead of meeting you up here." "Thank you Jack." "No, thank you Jill."

As evening approached so did Jack's anticipation, he knew what he wanted to do to Jill and was hoping she would agree to participate in what he had fantasized about earlier. It was close to dusk when Jill arrived at Jack's house. She had a little blue dress on that was loose and flowing but it was super short and he liked it.

As the warm air was blowing a light wind Jack noticed that the wind was going underneath Jill's dress and he could see what she was wearing. Nothing, no panties or no bra. Jack's dick was really getting hard now. As they came up on the steep hill Jack was ready to cum as well. He extended his hand for her to go by him and he would walk behind her up the hill. She went first and as the wind gently raised so did her dress. All of her ass was totally exposed and she knew it. She also knew he was looking and this was turning him on more. Her skin was so soft like butter and all he wanted to do was butter her muffin with his big dick that was beginning to drip cum.

When both of them made it up to the well with their pail to fetch their water Jack quickly dropped his pail took Jill's pail out of her hand, threw it to the side and grabbed her. He looked at her and kissed her. He turned her around to face the well bent her over and smacked her ass as hard as he could. He wasn't sure what her reaction would be.

He didn't know if she was going to hit him or push him down the steep hill they had just climbed. She turned around, looked at him and said, "do it again. Smack my ass as hard as you can. Make it red to look like a cherry. I know I'm going to holler but please don't stop. Only stop when you are ready to put your dick in my pussy, only stop when you are ready to fuck me Jack." Jack did what she requested, he smacked her as until it was red like a cherry and decided he wanted to see what her cherry tasted like. He turned her back around to him got on his knees, took his tongue and went around her clit. This was making Jill cum. It was running down her leg and as Jack saw it running down her leg he was catching it with his tongue. Jill was hollering so loud birds were flying out of trees but all she kept saying in the middle of her hollering was, "don't stop Jack, don't stop."

Jack finally did stop he looked up at Jill and told her to play with her wet hot pussy. "Jill put your finger in your pussy, let me see you moan, let me watch your face. Cum on yourself Jill, I want to see you pleasure yourself. Will you do that for me Jill? Make your pussy cum for me." "Ok Jack." Jill put her right leg up on a rock took her index finger and slid it into her wet hot pussy.

She started going in out with her finger as if Jack's dick was inside of her. He was watching her with this big smile on his face. As his dick was pulsating and ready to explode he took down his pants and his underwear turned her around to face the well bent her over and stuck his dick into her pussy from behind. He couldn't hold it any longer. He exploded all inside of her.

He took it out dripping wet, turned her back around gently pushing her down to her knees looking down at her he said, "Jill lick the cum off my dick. I want you to taste us Jill. Then suck my dick until I tell you to stop. I have more cum to put inside of you." Jill did what Jack said. She sucked his dick until it got hard again.

He stood her up turned her back around and stuck his dick back into her pussy slipped his hands up her body squeezing and pinching her titties. She was screaming by this time because she was on the verge of having an orgasm. She had never had one and then it came, she spurted and came all over his dick while it was inside of her. They were both sweating all over each other. Jack was kissing and licking Jill's neck as he was squirting his cum into her. When he got done he took a bucket of water emptied it all over her and as the cold water made her nipples even harder he drove his dick into her already soaked pussy once more.

After they were done fucking they got dressed fetched their water and was ready to walk back down the hill. Jill never looked at fetching water as a chore again. In fact, she looked forward to it every day as long as she knew Jack would be there and Jack was happy to help her out.

Eventually indoor plumbing was invented and Jill was pissed.

# A Lady Who Lived In A Shoe

There once was a lady who lived in a shoe she had so many children you would think she knew what to do. Stop having them! But she didn't and her house was overrun with children for years until one day she looked up and all of them had disappeared.

How quickly time had gone by and now this lady was left with a feeling of emptiness and being alone. She really didn't know what to do with herself.

She tried hanging out with her friends but that got boring to her. She wanted something more exciting. She wanted something to spice up her life. She decided to revisit some of the men she knew in high school but that didn't work. She went to dating websites but she didn't seem to like that.

She decided to leave it alone so one day when she was dropping off a package at the post office she saw this man standing in line waiting to have a package shipped as well. He tried to make small talk with her but she was ignoring him. He wasn't who she saw herself with. He was tall and lanky and to her he just looked goofy. He continued to try and have small talk with her but again she just ignored him.

When she was next in line she said thank you and walked past the man like he was invisible. A couple of weeks went by when she ran into him at the grocery store. She saw him stocking shelves.

She said to herself, "that figures, should have known he did a job like that." He saw her and politely smiled.

This time he did more than try and have a conversation with her he asked her out for coffee. She got kind of rude and said , "when on your 10 minute break?" He again just smiled and said, "No and by the way my name is Justice." "Did you say Justice, you don't look like a Justice." He replied, "my mother named me that because she taught me to treat everyone fair and with respect." "Ok Justice, my name is Suzette, sure lets have coffee sometimes."

"Well Suzette since I got your attention with coffee lets step it up and meet for dinner." Suzette engaged with him and said, "sure but can you afford it?" Again, Justice just smiled, got her number so he could come and pick her up. When he called her and got her address he arrived in a taxi. She was wondering to herself that their date was not going to go well at all but she refrained

from being a smart ass. She asked him when he got to the door "why did you take a cab? Where is your car? Do you drive?" He said, "Well, Suzette I thought we might try a little bistro I heard about out on the east coast." "What," said Suzette, "we need to fly there if he want to get there tonight." Justice said, "ok let's go and not waste any more time." She was puzzled but there was something about him that made her comfortable and she could really be herself and although she didn't believe him she went along with what she considered a bunch of bull.

The cab drove to the private airplane hanger and dropped them off. When they got out they were greeted by the pilot and copilot of a dual engine jet. "Good evening Justice, are you ready to take flight?" "Hello Brian, Yes I am, this is Suzette. Suzette these 2 men are my pilot and copilot." They went up the steps to the jet and were seated on butterscotch leather. She was thinking "wow my ass has never felt so good" then Suzette's mouth dropped and she said "your pilots?" "Yes Suzette, I make it a point to get to know all of the employees who work in my chain of grocery stores all across the nation. It's important to me as owner and CEO.

I like to be hands on and do whatever it takes to satisfy the customers and honestly they are not the only ones I would like to satisfy, I would very much like to satisfy you." She was blushing by this time and with the heat coming off the seat her pussy was getting just as hot. The steward walked up and said, "Hello Suzette would you like some wine?" "Yes please." She was sipping her wine and before you know it the jet had taken off in the air.

The flight was only going to take about an hour and a half and that was time for Justice to do what had been on his mine ever since his first encounter with her in the post office. He removed his seat belt, got up and went over to Suzette. He leaned down and started to whispering in her ear. "Suzette I very much want to slide your dress up right now, you smell so good, can I slide your dress up and take your panties off? Don't tell me, just shake your head yes or no." Suzette shuck her head yes and he did what he asked her. Her panties were soaked with her pussy juices. Then he whispered again and said "can I feel your wet hot pussy I can tell it's wet, I see the juices on you. Can I touch it? Don't say it just shake your head yes or no."

Again, she said motioned her head as a yes. He took two of his fingers and moved them over her clit and slid them up in her pussy. He could feel her pussy pulsating as she came all over his fingers. When he removed them they were white with her cum. He looked her cum off of his fingers. With a whisper he said, "now can I move my head down in position where I can gently take my tongue and lick it over your clit. Can I taste the juices that are flowing from your pussy? You smell so good. Then I want to take my tongue and push it as far as it can go up your pussy. I want you to squirt in my mouth. Don't hold back. Give me all you got."

He asked her the same question and of course she nodded with a yes. He got in position, took his tongue and moved it gently over her clit. She was cumming all over his tongue. He took his fingers spread her lips apart and licked on the inside and outside of her pussy as she breathed deep and moaned in pleasure.

It seemed like his entire face was in her pussy and although they were flying she really felt like she was floating on air. She had never experienced anything like this. In spite of all the children she had it was never this sexually stimulating. She wanted more. She grabbed the back of his head and pushed it into her pussy has much as she could.

He could tell she wanted more and he planned to give her more. He came up for air and said, "suck my dick Suzette, suck it long and hard." She obliged. She was new at this as well. She wasn't sure what to do. She read books and thought about the things her girlfriends suggested to her but she was still a little unsure of what to do but she did her best. He stood up took his pants down, pulled his dick out through his underwear and put his dick in her mouth. He was patient and guided her through the process of what to do. To her surprise she liked it and wanted to stay at it until she got it right. By this time they had been in the air for about an hour.

By this time both of their clothes were off. He picked her up put her legs over his shoulders had her dangling upside down and he drove his tongue deep into her wetness. She exploded inside of his mouth. She had never had an orgasm in her life. He allowed it to run down his face and all over his chest.

She just screamed, it was over, she couldn't hold it any longer. This was more than she could handle in all her years of living. She wanted more of what he could give her. She wanted to experience it all but there was no way. Both of them had just enough time to clean up before the jet was scheduled to land. This two hour flight seemed like a lifetime to Suzette.

They landed, got off the plane, and took a car to dinner. After dinner they went back to the airport, boarded the jet to head back home. Nothing happened but she was hoping she would get fucked on the way back. Treat it like an after dinner mint perhaps but nothing. He talked, he told her about who he was, how he travelled all the time but wanted to see her again.

He just didn't know when. He asked her about her life and what made her happy. After they landed she got off the plane and they said their goodbyes there. He had his driver take her home. After she arrived home she realized she had no way to get in touch with him. All she could think about was the evening she had with Justice. She had lived all those years in a space of close mindedness. She was closed off to new things, people, adventure and potential love. It was like trying to put a size 7 foot in a size 6 shoe. The foot will never fit in the shoe, it has no room to breathe and eventually she would have to either remove her foot or cut the shoe apart. The shoe was her mind; once she opened her mind life could begin.

About 6 weeks later she went to the post office to drop off a package when she heard this familiar voice whisper in her ear and this time she was the one who was smiling.

## PETER, PETER

**P**eter grew up with 8 brothers and sisters in a town where it was nothing but country but they always managed to have fun and make the best out of what they had. There were other children around them that they grew up with but of course as the years went by things changed.

Six of Peter's siblings moved away to either work or go off to college. Peter and his younger brother were left behind to tend to the pumpkin patch. Their parents were getting up in age but remained very active in the pumpkin field. Of course all of them loved pumpkin. Pumpkin pie, pumpkin bread, pumpkin seeds, you name it, if it was made with pumpkin they ate it. Peter ate pumpkin some much the girls who lived nearby gave him the nickname Peter, Peter, pumpkin eater.

Peter was okay with this when he was younger but the older he got he was setting his sights on something else. He was getting tired of going out to the pumpkin patch everyday getting a hard dick and having to masturbate.

One day Glenda was walking pass the pumpkin patch and noticed Peter out there working so she walked up the field to where he was and the first thing that came out of her mouth was Peter, Peter, pumpkin eater. Peter was looking at her with this disgusted look on his face. Just then he grabbed her and kissed her. She wasn't sure how to take it at first so she just kissed him back and before they knew it both of them was lying down in the pumpkin field kissing. Then he moved his hand up her shirt and under her bra and started squeezing her big titties.

"Glenda I'm tired of masturbating whenever I get a hard dick. I want some pussy Glenda. Do you want to help me or what?" Glenda said, "I can't help you today but maybe I can tomorrow. I better get home." He said "damn, okay".

So Peter was standing in the field with a hard dick once more when Sally was walking by. He called her name and asked her to come to where he was. When Sally walked up to him she looked down and noticed that his dick was hard. He grabbed Sally and kissed her. She didn't indulge, she just ran away. Peter was pissed that his dick was so hard and he couldn't get any pussy. No sooner than Sally had left Lucy was coming by.

Lucy was laid back, easygoing and really didn't care what people thought or said about her. She just enjoyed life. Peter started not to yell for Lucy but he did. He figured the third time was a charm. He did the same thing. He grabbed Lucy and kissed her. She kissed him back and kissed him hard. She found herself on the ground with him ready to get it on when she suddenly said, "Wait Peter." Peter was thinking, "damn she is getting ready to get up and leave me with the hard dick that is dripping cum as I think." Lucy said, "hold on Peter, don't worry I'm not leaving." Just then she stood up, pulled down her shorts, she was not wearing any underwear. She told Peter to get down on his knees and put his face in her pussy. This time he was a little taken back. He was usually the aggressor. He did what she wanted.

Lucy started talking to him while he was eating out her pussy. Lucy was saying, "Peter, Peter, you're a pussy eater. Forget what you heard about pumpkins, forget what you heard about seeds, and forget what you heard about breads and pies because my pussy is where you should be." She told Peter to keep eating her pussy until she had enough and when she did she let him up.

Then she got down on all fours in the field and told him to ride her like a bull rides a cow so he did. He fucked her as long as she wanted him to and told him "keep going, don't stop, you better not move." He did what she said because this was turning him on. He busted his cum all inside of her and she was not satisfied until he was done.

They both laid there when they were finished chewing on seeds and as they were laying there he wondered to himself what tomorrow would bring. Well tomorrow did come and he saw Glenda and Sally waking down the road. He figured they both talked about what happened the day before. Surprisingly no, he thought they would but they were waiting for him to call their names but in the field he just stood. He stood there and watched them walk by. He had this big smile on his face and this time when they spoke it, he didn't have a face of disgrace. They yelled to Peter once more and said "Peter, Peter, pussy eater. Forget what you heard about pumpkins, forget what you heard about seeds, and forget what you heard about breads and pies because my pussy is where you should be."

Peter yelled back and said well if that's the case where are you going? Glenda was curious and wanted to go back but didn't want to go back without Sally. So they both walked back and Peter asked Glenda what she wanted. Glenda said, "Oh Peter, I want you to be my pussy eater." So he obliged. Glenda pulled up her dress pulled her panties down laid down in the pumpkin field spread eagle and Peter went to town. Although without admitting it, it turned Sally on but once again she ran off. She was labeled the good girl. Peter just bided his time because he knew if Sally walked down that road enough times and sees him in the pumpkin patch she eventually is going to let Peter be her pussy eater to.

# GEORGY PORGY

Georgy Porgy was fine and nickel slick, Georgy Porgy was a pimp. He put his holes out on the block and expected to be paid in full when they were done fucking someone. He handled each hole with a stern hand. He let them know he would pull out the wire hanger and whoop their ass with it if the bitch didn't give him his money.

Georgy was so slick he even had a waiting list. You see Georgy was a player in the rawest form and it seemed every woman he laid eyes on he ended up fucking. There was something about him that women found irresistible.

He didn't fuck the holes on the block he fucked the holes that considered themselves classy and untouchable.

One evening as Mr. P pulled up to one of the most extravagant restaurants in the area he was greeted by the valet staff to park his car. The staff member happened to be a young woman who looked like she wanted to be fucked. "Excuse me sir, I need for you to leave your key in your ignition so I can park it." "I know sweetheart but I'd rather see where you are parking my car and then you can drive me back to the front door." "Yes sir, I can do that." "Don't call me sir, call me Mr. P. What's your name sweetheart?" "Heather is my name." "Well okay Heather, you ready for the ride of your life?" "Yes." She drove his car to the spot where it was going to be parked, put the gear in park and turned off the car.

George looked at Heather and said, "Heather, suck my dick. Suck my dick sweetheart. You know you want to." Before Heather knew it she was slobbering all over his dick, her pants and panties were down and Georgy P had 3 of his fingers in her young hot pussy. She was so tight she started crying from the pain and pleasure. He just kept saying, "you got it sweetheart, go deeper, you got it. Damn you may have a future in dick sucking but I'm not recruiting today."

After they were finished she drove him back to the front door, he got out of the car and walked inside the restaurant. He was taken to his table by the host and greeted by his wait staff. "Good evening sir, may I take your order?" "Yes baby, I'm sorry, I meant to call you by your name. Is that correct? Does your name tag say Tasty?" "Yes sir, that's my name." "Hmmmm I may have to see if you stand up to your name. In the meantime I'd like a scotch on the rocks." Tasty blushed as she took his drink order and walked away. When she returned with his drink he noticed that she walked toward the ladies room.

He sipped his drink stood up and started walking toward the ladies room. As a woman was coming out of the restroom he asked, "Is there anyone else in there? I'm not sure where my date is." "Oh sir there is one more person in there." "Thank you so much mamn." He saw an out of order sign by the door sat it in front of the restroom and went in. He washed his hands, washed off his dick, stood by the sink and waited for Tasty to come out of the stall.

When she opened the door and saw him standing there she was shocked. "Sir I believe you're in the wrong restroom." "On the contrary I want to see how Tasty you are, wash your pussy." Something in her could not resist him, she did what he requested. He told her to get up on the counter and lay down. He bent down over her and started licking her clit. As her pussy started flowing he said, "You are tasty, Tasty. Do you like being a waitress?"

"It's okay I am working here to help with school. I'm going to be a chemist." As she managed to speak those words while George was licking her clit and shoving his tongue into her pussy he suddenly stopped, got up and pointed for her to change position and lean over the counter. There was no warning. As soon as she bent over he rammed his huge masculinity into her. She started crying. The pain in her ass was absorbed by the juices flowing out of her pussy. The cum was running down her legs and she loved it.

When he finished he cleaned himself up, went to the door, turned around, looked at Tasty and said, "Hurry Tasty, you still need to take my order (paused). I also don't want you to lose your job." She cleaned herself up and made it back to his table. He placed his order and ate very well after his encounters. When he was leaving he left Tasty's tip on the table that was quite substantial which left her speechless and a little misty eyed.

When George approached the door to leave the restaurant Heather pulled up in his car and handed him the keys. He put a large bill in her hand and gave her a quick wink. She stood there with watery eyes as he pulled off.

Before he went home he stopped by the bar close to his house and while talking to some of his colleagues' one asked him, "George how you do it?"

George replied, "I'm Georgy Porgy big and fine, fuck girls so hard I make them cry. When the other boys thought they were going to play I just looked at them and said I fucked your girl today. Don't be fooled by my physique I got a big dick that's what your girl needs. So don't get mad when I stroke my tongue and lay my pipe, take some points and fuck your girl then roll the fuck over and say good night."

www.ingramcontent.com/pod-product-compliance
Lightning Source LLC
Chambersburg PA
CBHW020657180626
46816CB00003B/1335